14¢ RL 10
PrinFiL

D1538105

AUG 1 9 2011

_____   _____ _____
(my name)   (date)   (years old)

Little Chief and Mighty Gopher: The Pemmican Frenzy

Written by: Victor Lethbridge
Illustrated by: Ben Crane
TATANKA PRODUCTIONS

Little Chief and Mighty Gopher:
The Pemmican Frenzy

Educational Partners*

Shell Canada Energy
Syncrude Canada
Enbridge Inc.
All Nations Optimist Club of Medicine Hat, AB
Bonavista Petroleum Ltd.
Devon Canada
Japan Canada Oil Sands (JACOS)
Fairborne Energy Trust
Brett Binder Leadership Fund **
Taylor Guitars ***

We acknowledge the support of the Canada Council for the Arts which last year invested $20.1 million in writing and publishing throughout Canada.

Nous remercions de son soutien le Conseil des Arts du Canada, qui a investi 20,1 millions de dollars l'an dernier dans les lettres et l'édition à travers le Canada.

Canada Council   Conseil des Arts
for the Arts   du Canada

*Many thanks to our Educational partners, whose generosity has allowed us to give workshops and provide books to youth in many Aboriginal communities through Aboriginal Youth TREK Wellness Society.

** Established in honour of a remarkable young man, the Brett Binder Leadership Fund carries on Brett's legacy of caring, kindness and unconditional acceptance of today's youth. On his behalf, books are donated to hospitals and youth organizations across Canada so children can discover joy and hope despite adversities in their lives.

*** When on tour, Victor plays Taylor Guitars and wishes to thank Taylor for their support.***

For Dorothy, my wife, partner, and dream maker. With Love - Victor

To Howie and Anna Crane, who never told their son "That's a nice drawing.
Now go out and get a real job!" - Ben

Published and Produced by Storyteller Media and Tatanka Productions

Text copyright © 2010 by Victor Lethbridge
Illustrations copyright © 2010 by Ben Crane
All rights reserved.

No part of this publication may be reproduced in whole or in part, or stored in a retrieval system, or
transmitted in any form, or by any means, electronic, mechanical, photocopying, recording, or otherwise,
without written permission from the publisher. For information regarding permission, write to:
Tatanka Productions Box 10, Rolling Hills, AB T0J 2S0
www.TatankaWorkshops.com

FIRST EDITION   Printed in China through Colorcraft Ltd, Hong Kong.
The illustrations of this book were pencil drawn then scanned and digitally painted.
The type is set in 16 point Times Roman

Summary: Discover what happens when a young aboriginal boy's friendship with a gopher turns everyone's life upside down!
Editors: Dorothy Lethbridge, Lauri Seidlitz and our community of contributors as listed on our web page.
Marketing by: Dorothy Lethbridge and Ellie Hirch Publicist: Ron Wall

Library and Archives Canada Cataloguing in Publication
Lethbridge, Victor, 1964-
Little chief and mighty gopher : the pemmican frenzy / by Victor
Lethbridge ; illustrated by Ben Crane ; edited by Dorothy Lethbridge.

ISBN 978-0-9866738-0-1

I. Crane, Ben II. Lethbridge, Dorothy, 1957- III. Title.

PS8623.E923L58 2010   jC813'.6   C2010-904869-5

Many moons ago, there was a young boy named Snow Cloud. He lived in a peaceful tipi camp nestled in the hills on the edge of the vast prairie.

Snow Cloud's father was the tribal leader. His name was Chief Red Stone. Spending time with his son was difficult because Chief Red Stone was very busy looking after his people.

Snow Cloud's mother was Gentle Willow. She picked chokecherries and other berries, and she dried meat. She made the best pemmican in the camp. She smiled a lot, but Gentle Willow's heart was heavy because her son did not have any friends.

Snow Cloud couldn't run like the other children. One of his feet lagged behind the other, and Snow Cloud struggled to keep up. Sometimes the children teased and laughed at him.

He longed for a friend.

Snow Cloud loved to spend his days watching the prairie and all its animals.

When he looked to the east, he saw the deep coulees where his mother picked her berries. That's where the hawks had their nests.

When he looked to the south, he saw the winding river with its steep cliffs and hidden crevices. That's where the coyotes had their dens.

When he looked to the west, he saw the wide-open prairie. That's where the buffalo roamed.

When he looked to the north, he saw the rolling hills. That's where the gophers played, including a very special one named Mighty Gopher.

Early one afternoon, the young boys were out exploring and playing in the hills. One of the boys tripped Snow Cloud, who fell into the coarse grass and called out, "Wait for me!"

But the boys ran on.

Looking back, they taunted, "You're not Snow Cloud, you're S-L-O-W Cloud."

Snow Cloud's eyes brimmed with tears as he saw the boys disappear over the hills, leaving him all alone.

Suddenly, Snow Cloud heard a high-pitched whistle. Turning his head, he spotted Mighty Gopher peeking out of his hole. Quickly, the gopher ducked down. Then, cautiously, he peeked out again.

Soon they were playing hide-and-seek, and Snow Cloud forgot about being lonely.

Before long, other gophers were playing too, popping in and out of their holes and darting back and forth from behind the sagebrush.

Nearby, the buffalo curiously watched. Snow Cloud spotted them and said, "Come play with us!"

The buffalo gladly joined in, and they all played together until the sun began to dip below the horizon.

Darkness followed and Snow Cloud reluctantly went back to the tipi camp. He had no idea that Mighty Gopher followed him home.

While everyone was sitting around the campfire telling stories, Mighty Gopher snuck into Chief Red Stone's tipi. There, in a skin pouch, he discovered Gentle Willow's pemmican.

It was delicious! He couldn't get enough of it!

He hurried back to the other gophers, carrying some of the scrumptious pemmican to share.

The next day, the gophers invaded the tipi camp to get more pemmican.

There were gophers everywhere, scurrying between tipis, overturning things, and creating a terrible mess throughout the camp.

Round and round they ran. SKWEET, SKWEET, SKWEET. Up and down, through and around, SKWEET, SKWEET, SKWEET.

Snow Cloud threw back his head in laughter.

Chief Red Stone shook his fist in anger. "These gophers have to go. They're causing a frenzy and the pemmican is disappearing."

Chief Red Stone did not like what the gophers were doing. NOT ONE BIT!

He called the Elders forward and asked, "How do we get rid of all these gophers?"

The Elders thought and talked and talked and thought. Eventually they came up with an idea.

"Let's bring in …"

"HAWKS!"

So the Elders brought in lots of hawks … old hawks, young hawks, big hawks, and little hawks. All the gophers ran away, but the hawks stayed. The hawks created even more commotion, and now they started eating the pemmican too!

Round and round they flew. FLAP, FLAP, FLAP. Up and down, through and around, FLAP, FLAP, FLAP.

Snow Cloud squealed with delight.

Chief Red Stone stomped his foot. "The hawks are eating our winter food."

He did not like what the hawks were doing. NOT ONE BIT!

Again, Chief Red Stone called on the Elders. "How do we get rid of all these hawks?"

The Elders thought and talked and talked and thought. Eventually they came up with an idea.

"Let's bring in …"

"COYOTES!"

So the Elders brought in lots of coyotes . . . old coyotes, young coyotes, big coyotes, and little coyotes. The hawks flew away, but the coyotes stayed. The coyotes caused turmoil – they pounced on and devoured any pemmican in sight.

Round and round they ran. YIP - YIP, H-O-W-L. Up and down, through and around, YIP - YIP, H-O-W-L.

Snow Cloud rolled on the ground in laughter, but Chief Red Stone shook his finger. "These hungry coyotes are eating all our pemmican."

He did not like what the coyotes were doing. NOT ONE BIT!

Once again, Chief Red Stone called on the Elders. "How do we get rid of all these coyotes?"

The Elders thought and talked and talked and thought. Eventually they came up with an idea.

"Let's bring in …"

"BUFFALO!"

So the Elders brought in lots of buffalo . . . old buffalo, young buffalo, big buffalo, and little buffalo. The buffalo snorted and kicked, and pushed and shoved until all the coyotes were gone, but then there were buffalo everywhere! They caused a terrible ruckus and made a great big mess.

Round and round they ran. STOMP, STOMP, STOMP. Up and down, through and around, STOMP, STOMP, STOMP.

Snow Cloud doubled over in laughter, but Chief Red Stone just shook his head.

He did not like what the buffalo were doing. NOT ONE BIT!

One more time, Chief Red Stone called on the Elders and pleaded with them, "What do we do with all the buffalo?"

The Elders thought and talked and talked and thought.

No one had any ideas.

While the Elders were still pondering, Snow Cloud slowly crept forward. Taking a deep breath, he boldly spoke up, "Bring back the gophers!"

The Elders could not believe their ears. "Why would you want those gophers back? That's how this whole frenzy started in the first place!"

But he knew what he was doing. Snow Cloud, his friend Mighty Gopher, and all the other gophers gathered their buffalo friends together.

Snow Cloud pointed out to the buffalo, "You chased away the coyotes, but now you're wrecking our tipi camp and my people will suffer. Life on the prairie is balanced and every animal has its place, including you, the buffalo, who belong on the wide-open prairie."

The buffalo agreed. They didn't like being in the tipi camp. They followed Mighty Gopher and the other gophers back to where they belonged.

As all the animals left, the people raised their arms and cheered.

Marshall County Public Library
@ Hardin
Hardin, KY 42048

Chief Red Stone proclaimed, "We must have a celebration!"

After the feast and dancing, Chief Red Stone stepped into the warm glow of the firelight and called Snow Cloud forward. "Because you used your special gift to reason with the animals, you brought harmony, balance and tranquility back to our tipi camp. From now on you will be known as Little Chief."

Gentle Willow smiled fondly.

Chief Red Stone rewarded his son with a very special feather, which an Elder put into Little Chief's hair for all to see.

The other children looked at Little Chief with a new-found respect. They wanted to be his friend and were sorry they had ever made fun of him.

Little Chief now had lots of friends, but he never forgot his first friend, Mighty Gopher.

They remained best friends forever.

Many thanks to the following for their guidance and input towards the cultural and traditional aspects of this book:
- Chief David Ogle, Wood Mountain Lakota First Nation, Saskatchewan
- Patricia Littlechild, Executive Director of Maskwachees Cultural College, Hobbema, Alberta

Chief David Ogle comments on Lakota/Sioux cultural traditions:

"To see a children's book that so accurately depicts Lakota culture is such a good thing, especially when the message of the story makes you smile when you read it."

Why We Say Buffalo not Bison:

"There are two reasons. Most important, the Lakota people have always been known as the 'The Buffalo People.' As well, bison is the scientific name of the North American buffalo. When the First Nations people started to speak English, they referred to them as buffalo which we still say today."

About Name Changing:

"A new name is given to a person after a significant event takes place, like a feat of courage, much like what happened to Snow Cloud. The new name would reflect their special gift or ability. For Snow Cloud, he would have been given a name such as 'He Walks with the Four Legged' because of his ability to interact with the animals."

"As you can imagine, it would have been a challenge to give this book that title, so they decided to stay with Little Chief."

About The Four Directions:

"The Lakota Way is to refer to the four geographic directions starting at the East, then moving South, West, and finally North. The colours representing the four directions in the Lakota Medicine Wheel are yellow, white, black, and red, respectively."

HARMONY BALANCE TRANQUILITY

HARMONY BALANCE TRANQUILITY

About Victor Lethbridge: Over the years, Victor Lethbridge has developed many skills and talents. Musician, storyteller, motivational speaker and, now with the publication of his first book *Little Chief and Mighty Gopher: The Pemmican Frenzy*, author can be added to his list of accomplishments.

A musician by trade, Victor plays a wide variety of instruments, including guitar, banjo, mandolin, drums, and bass. He also records and produces music for himself and other artists.

A member of Sitting Bull's Canadian reserve, Wood Mountain Lakota First Nation, Victor focuses his time and energy helping Canada's Aboriginal youth through his interactive workshops.

Each workshop incorporates music, video, and storytelling to address the critical issues of how to prevent bullying, build self-esteem, and develop essential leadership skills.

Playing music as part of a youth workshop

Victor's Lakota name, as given to him by his grandfather, William Lethbridge, is *Tatanka Ocokanyan,* which means "Middle Bull."

About Ben Crane: As an accomplished, award-winning artist and musician, Ben Crane exemplifies the values of the western way of life. He is a family man, is Alberta raised, and has been honing his craft since he was a boy.

Today you'll find Ben's work in magazines,

books, on Leanin' Tree cards, and at western festivals and concert venues across North America.

There you can hear him performing original tunes and old favourites of the western style music Ben loves so much.

Learn more at www.bencrane.com.

Check us out at for more information at www.TatankaWorkshops.com

- Workshop touring/booking information
- Words to the "Little Chief" song
- Pemmican recipe (modern day version)
- Lesson plans on bullying prevention
- Gopher and buffalo facts
- 4 pictures to colour
- Ron Papandrea's historical account: *The Foreign Policy of Sitting Bull and the War of 1876.*

"The Lakota Sioux Arriving at Wood Mountain, Saskatchewan"

William Lethbridge, Victor's grandfather, depicts the arrival of the Lakota Sioux in Canada with this beautiful painting entitled "The Sioux Arriving at Wood Mountain". This can be seen on permanent display at Wood Mountain Post Provincial Park. Picture used with permission of Saskatchewan Tourism, Parks, Culture & Sport.

Following the defeat of the 7th US Cavalry lead by General George A. Custer at the Battle of Little Big Horn in June of 1876, Chief Sitting Bull and his Hunkpapa chiefs lead nearly 5,000 of their people north. They crossed the Canada/US border, which the Lakota called the "Medicine Line", to distance themselves from the American cavalry.

The Lakota settled in the Wood Mountain area. At that time there were more Lakota in Canada than there were Europeans living in the region between Winnipeg and the Rocky Mountains.

The Lakota, as with Canada's other First Nations, were facing scarce food resources with fewer buffalo remaining. It was ultimately starvation that drove most of them back to the United States where they settled on reservations.

Among those having made the trek north to Canada was a young girl of 12 or 13. Her name was Crossed Eagle Quills (Julia Lethbridge). She is Victor's great grandmother. She was one of the about 250 who remained in Canada. In 1910 the Canadian government granted this group a small reserve in Wood Mountain.

Today, the legacy and cultural traditions of the Lakota live on in the lives of generations of descendants, many of whom are members of Wood Mountain Lakota First Nation.

* Excerpts taken from Ron Papandrea's historical account, *The Foreign Policy of Sitting Bull and the War of 1876*. Special thanks to Ron for his invaluable assistance. To read Ron's concise and complete report go to www.TatankaWorkshops.com.

* For a more complete history of the Lakota in Canada, read Ron's book "They Never Surrendered: The Lakota Sioux Band That Stayed in Canada".

HARMONY   BALANCE   TRANQUILITY

About Pemmican

Buffalo meat was probably the most important part of the Lakota diet. In fact, the buffalo provided much more than meat. The hide provided clothing and shelter and the bones were made into tools. Absolutely nothing went to waste.

The Plains First Nations people were nomadic and followed the buffalo herds. They needed a way to be able to preserve buffalo meat for times when fresh meat wasn't available. Also, they needed a light, easily moved source of food.

Here's what they did. First, they cut the meat into very thin strips and hung it to dry across sinew lines, either from a tipi or on wooden racks. The dry meat, which was called jerky, was used to make soups, stews or pemmican.

Here's how a soup or stew was made. First, they made a sack from a buffalo's stomach suspended from sticks. Jerky and water went into the sack, followed by red-hot stones from the campfire. The stones made the water boil and cooked the meat. Then, if available, wild vegetables such as turnips and onions were added, along with sage to season.

Victor's great grandmother, Crossed Eagle Quills (Julia Lethbridge) with children Kate & Jim, drying meat between tents.

Sometimes the jerky was made into pemmican, which was put in a buffalo skin bag to be carried on trips or stored as a buried cache for winter use or times of little food. The cache would be dug up at a later date for others to eat or for when the camp came around again. Meat preserved this way could be stored for years.

To make pemmican, jerky was pounded with a rock until it became a powder. The powder was mixed with melted fat and dried berries, like chokecherries, which were also pounded into a powder, pits and all.

A chunk of pemmican the size of the palm of a hand, was the equivalent of a small roast and would have enough sustenance to last a day. Even though a small amount was eaten, drinking water would make them feel full because it expanded in their stomachs.

TRADITIONS CULTURE HISTORY

Aboriginal Translations by:
Bev Johnson - Lakota Sioux
Darrell Royal - Blackfoot
Bruce Cutknife - Cree

Blackfoot

friend	nii taak ka wa
father	ninna
mother	ni ksista
east	pii nu po sti
south	ahma ska po tsi
west	a mii to tsi
north	a pa to so tsi
gopher	oomah ko ka ta
hawk	po ksi pii ta
coyote	a pii sii
buffalo	ii nii

Cree

friend	nitotem
father	nohtawi
mother	nikawi
east	sakastenohk
south	apihtakisikanohk
west	pahkisimohtahk
north	kiwetinohk
gopher	apisicanikwacas
hawk	apsicikihis
coyote	mescacakan
buffalo	paskwaw mostos

Lakota Sioux

friend	ḉóla
father	até
mother	iná
east	wíhinaṗa
south	itókagata
west	wiyóhpeyata
north	wazíyata
gopher	wahíŋkeya
hawk	cetáŋ
coyote	šuŋgmánitu
buffalo	tatáŋka

Marshall County Public Library
@ Hardin
Hardin, KY 42048

HARRY'S SONG

LILLIAN HOBAN

HARRY'S SONG

GREENWILLOW BOOKS
NEW YORK

Copyright © 1980 by Lillian Hoban. All rights reserved. No part of this book may be reproduced or utilized in any form or by any means, electronic or mechanical, including photocopying, recording or by any information storage and retrieval system, without permission in writing from the Publisher. Published by Greenwillow Books, A Division of William Morrow & Company, Inc., 105 Madison Avenue, New York, N.Y. 10016
The full-color art was reproduced from watercolor paintings. Designed by Ava Weiss
Printed in the United States of America   First Edition   1 2 3 4 5 6 7 8 9 10

Library of Congress Cataloging in Publication Data
Hoban, Lillian.   Harry's song.   Summary: Harry's contribution to the rabbits' winter provisions is unusual but not unappreciated.   [1.   Rabbits—Fiction]   I. Title   PZ7.H635Har   [E]
78-31712   ISBN 0-688-80220-6   ISBN 0-688-84220-8 lib. bdg.

FOR ESTA

The long fall shadow crept over the hill. It covered the rock where Harry Rabbit sat quietly singing. It chilled his toes and cooled his nose.

"Hurry, Harry," called his mother, Mrs. Rabbit. "It is getting late."

Harry didn't move.

"One hot, hot golden
summer day,"

sang Harry softly.

"The good green smell
of sweet warm grass."

"That's a lovely song, Harry," said Mrs. Fieldmouse as she hurried past. "Come along, children," she called. Five fat little Fieldmouse children came up the hill pulling a large basket of fall seeds.

"What are you singing?" they asked.

> *"The hazy, lazy rich
> ripe taste of August,"*

sang Harry.

> *"Bees buzzing in the
> honey-heavy air."*

"That's a summertime song, Harry," cried the
little Fieldmouse children. "It's fall now."

They pushed the basket into the hole where
Mrs. Fieldmouse stood waiting.

"That Harry is such a dreamer," said Mrs. Fieldmouse to her husband. "He hasn't even started to get ready for winter."

"Harry is a dumb bunny," said Mr. Fieldmouse. "He doesn't know enough to come in out of the cold." And Mr. Fieldmouse stored all the seeds his children had brought home in a large bin.

The fall shadow crept higher over the hill.
But Harry did not move. A cold wind ruffled his
fur. It blew in his ears and stirred his whiskers.

"Hurry home, Harry," called his mother from
the burrow below. "It is getting very late."

Harry sat very still, singing softly.

"Red roses in the garden,
black-eyed susans on the hill."

"No time to be singing, Harry," said old
Mr. Chipmunk as he came hurrying past.
Mr. Chipmunk's cheeks were stuffed with seeds.
He had seeds in his pockets and seeds in his
paws and a sack full of wheatgrass on his back.

"Time to get ready for winter," puffed Mr.
Chipmunk. "Time to store food for the cold
days ahead."

"*Rows of leafy lettuces
just rabbit-high and tender,*"

sang Harry.

"*Plump pods of sweet peas
climbing on the vine.*"

"Now, Harry," said Mr. Chipmunk, "that's a very nice song, but you really should think of your folks. They need more than a song to carry them through the winter."

Harry didn't move. He sat there in the wind and the cold of the late fall evening and sang:

> "And in daisy-deep meadows
>   a song-bird trills
>   and under the fern
>   a young rabbit sits still."

"Well," said Mr. Chipmunk, "you sure are a funny little bunny, Harry. It's a good thing all your brothers are hard-working rabbits or you and your family would go hungry all winter." Old Mr. Chipmunk shook his head and hurried off.

The long fall shadow darkened into night.
A thin new moon shone softly on the rock
where Harry sat.

"Harry," called Mrs. Rabbit. "Do come
home. It is very late."

Harry didn't move. He sat very still.
Deep deep inside, so no one could hear, he sang
his song.

A little brown bat came flitting by. He
swooped low over Harry and cried, "Winter is
coming! Winter is coming! Time to fatten up
for the long cold ahead."

Harry didn't move.

The little brown bat darted and dipped
in the dark of the night. "Harry," cried the little
brown bat, "bring home some grain, bring
home some greens, or you and your folks will
grow thin thin thin in the cold and the
snow of winter!"

Harry sat very still with his eyes closed.
Deep deep inside so no one could hear he
remembered summer and sang his song.

The little brown bat scooped up a moth and
headed for home. "Harry," he called, "won't
you bring home some bark, won't you bring
home some twigs? Won't you bring your folks
a little SOMETHING?"

Harry was very quiet. He just sat in
the wind and the cold and silently sang his
summertime song.

"Oh, you are a bothersome bumbling bunny!"
cried the little brown bat.

And he flew into his hollow tree to hole up
for the winter.

"Harry," called Mrs. Rabbit, "where are you, Harry? Your brothers are all here. We miss you, Harry. Please come home."

Harry opened his eyes and jumped off the rock and hopped down the hill and straight into the den where his mother and brothers were waiting.

One of his brothers
was sorting some grain.

And one of his brothers
was sorting some greens.

One of his brothers was storing some bark,
and one of his brothers was storing some twigs.

"Here's Harry!" they cried, "and he hasn't
brought anything home for winter."

"Yes I have," said Harry.
And he sang his song.

"Oh, Harry," said his mother, "how lovely! You've brought home the song of a perfect summer day to carry us through the winter. You are a honey of a bunny!" And she hugged him very hard.